ERIN MAY KELLY

THE
EVERYDAY CIRCUS

ISBN : 978-1-911424-52-9
SKU/ID: 9781911424529

No part of this book can be reproduced in any form or by written, electronic or mechanical, including photocopying, recording, or by any information retrieval system without written permission in writing by the author.

ORIGINAL COVER:
Title: THE EVERYDAY CIRCUS
Artist: Fabio Perla
Technique: drawing, sanguigna pencil on wood
Size: 66.8 x 50.8 cm
Year: 2016

Book design by: Wolf
Preface by:
Editor Monica Turoni
and
Writer Erin May Kelly

Publishing Company:
Black Wolf Edition & Publishing Ltd.
2 Glebe Place, Burntisland KY3 0ES, Scotland
www.blackwolfedition.com

Copyright © 2016 by Black Wolf Edition & Publishing Ltd.
All rights reserved. - First Printing: 2016
Second Edition 2017

This book if for my amazing parents who always encourage my ridiculous dreams and never told me to quit and get a real job. And for Oisin and Ninian who helped by being wonderful.
For my incredible friends who are so important.
Especially Kellie — words, what are they?
And for anyone who reads these stories, thank you.

PREFACE

Touching, unexpected, revealing short stories about life experiences shown with realism, sarcasm and personal touch.
The reader will find himself as an external viewer or the principal character of each story.

The book cover is created by Fabio Perla with sanguigna pencil on wood.
The work was born from the inspiration of the stories contained in the book of the same name. The hand represents the profound soul of the human being that contains all the state of mind (the eye) we live everyday in the path of our life. The life is like a circus full of strong emotions, attractions but also tensions and fears. The lock and the key are the connection between our soul and the real life.

Monica Turoni
(The Editor)

INTRODUCTION

Amazing, incredible and soul destroying things happen to us all. We can get so caught up in chasing glory and fame that we forget how magical everyday life is.
This book is about love, death, young mums, breakups, feminism and more. It is about the amazing things that happen to us every day.
Welcome to The Everyday Circus.

Erin May Kelly
(Writer)

LET'S GO DOWN TO THE WOODS

Someone asked me to write a love story. They said that my words are too dark and my life needs more light.

I don't know how to write love stories because I don't want one.

I want a story with decaying castles and monsters that look like they crawled out of children's nightmares. I want books that make your skin crawl and stories that make you afraid of falling asleep.

If that doesn't scare you, then let's write a story together.

Let's go down to the woods. Let's go explore somewhere dark. Somewhere haunted by everyone who never lived there. The ghosts of people who were too scared of the dark to ever set foot inside it. I'm not scared of the dark. I'm not scared of the things that live inside it either.

I've had a lot of Princes trying to save me from it, they don't understand that it comforts me. I need my darkness. You need the sky to be dark so you can see the stars.

I'm not the girl who sings with the birds and I never will be.

I don't want to be saved by a Prince.

But you're not a Prince anyway. You're the boy who ran away with the circus. You taught yourself to juggle when you were meant to be learning to fight and maybe that's why this work. Because I don't need you to fight for me. I don't need you to save me. I just need you to be there while I save myself.

I have my own sword and I have killed more dragons than story books can remember. I climbed out of the tower without help and ate a whole orchard of poisoned apples.

I don't want gold. I want something that you built with your own hands. Build me a house of cards and I will live inside it like it's a palace. I don't want treasure. I want you to tell me about every part of yourself that you're scared of. I want you to love me when I'm not loveable. I want you to admire of me for killing all the dragons that tried to kill me first.

I can't write you a love story. Because I need my story to be more than love. I need magic and adventure. I need to be the girl who saves herself. But I can write you a fairy tale, and maybe somewhere in the middle, we can fall in love.

MONSTERS

I grew up watching horror movies and reading ghost stories. I was a fearless child and became so immune to monsters that when I was older, I couldn't even see when they were standing in front of me.

We're told that evil lies inside ugly creatures with rotting skin and sharp teeth. But evil can live inside beautiful boys with kind smiles and messy hair.

I never checked under my bed at night, I didn't need to. The monster did not sleep there, he slept on top of the bed, with his arms wrapped around me, breathing fire down my neck.

I know there is not such thing as a perfect man. But there is a difference between men who break hearts and men who break bones. His mistakes painted my body purple.

The first time he did it, we both stood in shock. His apology lasted a month, decorated with bouquets of expensive flowers and cooked meals. The second apology only lasted a week. The bouquets got smaller and the dinners fewer.

When his third apology came, the flowers he brought were dead.

I should have burned down the house and ran for my life, instead I sank back into our coffin shaped bed and forgave him for every part of me he killed.

One night he threw a plate over my head, smashing a mirror and damming us to seven years bad luck.

I screamed that I had used all my bad luck up already, being the girl that gets woken up by his whisky breath and rough hands.

He hit me with all of his fury and I stumbled. Falling back into the bathroom I spluttered violently, covering the sink in a mosaic of broken teeth and blood.

That night he wiped the blood from my face so lovingly that I forgot it was him who put it there.

He tucked my hair behind my ear. His hands were cold and his eyes were cold and his heart was cold.

I pretended it was normal to scrub blood off the walls. To speak with missing teeth and see through swollen eyes. I don't know how to tell you what it feels like to love someone who is killing you.

Every time his eyes glowed red, I looked away, telling myself I could not see his pointed fangs and forked tongue. He was not evil, he was the boy who kissed my forehead and was afraid of spiders.

I only saw the side of him that lit up the sky, refusing to see the darkness, the part of him that was real. I was in love with someone who did not exist.

I lived in a tower kept secret from the rest of the world. The people outside would not understand. If they saw my face they would bring pitchforks to our door, ready to behead the beast who split my skin.

I can't remember much of the night I left. Only how the staircase felt against my spine, and his screams as I fell.

I was taken away with blinding lights and sirens. People who loved me cried and stroked my face.

Even when I woke up, his was the first name I asked for.

Doctors stuck my bones back together and rubbed cream into

my blackened skin. But he broke something much deeper than bone. Something the doctors couldn't reach.

They could not fix the way I flinched every time the nurse lifted his hand.

The fearless girl was replaced with a nervous wreck, afraid of the dark, jumping at loud noises. You can't stitch trust back together.

Now I check under my bed every night. I keep the lights on and don't dangle my feet outside the covers. I never believed in monsters, until it was too late, he had already bitten me.

Erin May Kelly

THE BREAKUP LETTER

This is a letter to tell you that you didn't win. Maybe you think that me writing to you means that you still have a hold on me, and maybe you do for now. I can only heal as quickly as a human being can after all.

But even though the dull pain of missing you is still there, I can see through the fog and I stamped on those rose tinted glasses.

You took every single tiny shard of insecurity I had and sharpened it so you would always have something to stab me with when I tried to stand up to you.

You knew exactly how to pierce between ribs with things that would get stuck in my skin, so late at night I sat trying to pick them out but somehow only pushed them further in.

It took so long to unlearn all the ways you taught me to hate myself.

You spat so much venom at me it took months to suck the poison out and even now it's still stuck in my bloodstream. I sat for days stitching your broken skin back together. When your wounds healed I held out my mine so you could do the same. You wrinkled your nose as you looked at me, you said you never asked me for anything, then left me alone to try and fix the destruction you caused.

I can still taste your lying tongue. Your mouth is full of poison but mine is full of razorblades. When you kiss me I will leave a taste of blood that you cannot get rid of.

The next girl you sleep beside will hear you breathe my name in your sleep, as your nightmares are fuelled by what you did to me. You made a mistake when you assumed that small creatures don't have sharp teeth. I have bitten flesh and clawed my way out of the dirt to stay alive. Just because you pushed me into the ground does not mean I'll stay there.

I saved your life when everyone abandoned you. I pulled you out of Hell even though it burned my arms. I held your hand as you taught yourself to walk again. Carefully handing you brick after brick until you had rebuilt your life. That's when you left. When I was in Hell you just left me there. When I had to teach myself how to walk again, you didn't even offer me your hand. You left me alone in the lowest, darkest place I've ever been. But already, I have started to pull myself out of the dark. I might not be able to see the light yet, but I finally believe it's there.

I might be the one hurting right now, but I will get better and I will get stronger and I will climb mountains that you can't even see the top of. I will fight through this even on the nights when my body shakes and my thoughts sting.

You don't know how to love and that is how you lose. You will always be the one who broke something beautiful.

After all this, I will continue to love, and that is how I win. Because I will not let my experience with evil destroy my belief in good.

I will always be the girl who fought off the vultures when you were left for dead.

I will always be the girl who you broke but could not kill.

BLACK LUNGS

We're warned that breathing in too much smoke will blacken our lungs. We're never warned that breathing in too much of one person can do the same thing to our hearts. So you learned the hard way. That's why you treat people like cigarettes – something to hold at parties and drunk summer nights, but never let too far into your system. You need to stop trying to quit people. I know quitting seems too hard to go through more than once.

It made you shaky and sweaty, waking up in the night craving something you can't taste any more. So you covered yourself in nicotine patches. A different one every night, giving you a rush without the commitment. Then you ripped them off before they could leave a mark on your skin. Never letting them stay in time for breakfast.

You think you know what will happen if you let them stay. A rush of short term pleasure followed by a long term sickness. You've forgotten that not everyone will make you sick. Some things that form inside your organs are not chemicals or fumes. Sometimes it's hard to tell the difference between falling ill and falling in love, they both make you choke and keep you up at night.

You know that trust is only broken by people you love, never by people you keep at a safe distance. So if you hold a person at arms length then they can't burn you. They can't get inside and learn all the dark parts of you just to leave again.

There is nothing more terrifying than feeling safe. Safety can crumble and happiness can stop and people can leave. You live in fear of worst case scenarios. You live with the belief that history will repeat itself and it's crippling you.

Your tongue has scorch marks on it from when you trusted a bit too much. So you clamp it between your teeth instead of asking someone to stay. Because you met someone new and could feel the addiction rising inside you. You wake up and you want them, you fall asleep and you want them and it tastes too much like that thing you had to quit before.

Smiling looks really good on you. Your face shape doesn't suit sadness. I know it started of as a fashion accessory but it became an addiction. Addictions destroy lives and tear down people. Everyone watched as you let yourself become sick. You got thinner and slower and became nothing more than side affects of addiction.

Your bones are not as brittle as you think they are. If someone's smile knocks you sideways then let it. It doesn't hurt every time you fall.

You are stronger than the sickness you lived through.

I know trusting again is scarier than the thought of being alone.

But one day someone will kiss all the parts of yourself that you're not sure how to love. Let them stay. Let them crawl under your blankets and into the safe little place you built yourself. Breathe them in.

YOU AFTER HIM

This is how I will make you leave. I will tell you about the man who you will never be.

You are a too beautiful person for me to break. So I will make you leave.

I will push you away so hard it will bruise your insides.

Because I will never stop counting all the ways which you are not him. The only problem is, you are the first person I've met who I didn't want to be him. You are the first person who didn't have his eyes. You had your own. My stomach did a flip when I looked at you and saw blue instead of brown.

But this is a home I built for him, not you. The walls are painted his favourite colour. Dark forest green will always mark his territory. His photograph is next to my bed and he can see when you sleep there.

I will make you leave by telling you that he still lives here. Sometimes when I brush my teeth he stands behind me. The last shirt he wore hangs next to my dresses. His boots are in the wardrobe, caked in mud from a walk that I shouldn't have taken for granted. You say that you are not trying to take his place. I know you are in love.

But you can't be in love with me because I haven't been me for years. You are in love with a mask. You are in love with the way I puppeteer my body to make it act alive.

Every time I push you out the door, you knock and wait. You wait patiently for me to be something that I can never be for you.

I burned all my bridges so you swam to me instead.

You offered to buy me flowers to give to him. I can't give him flowers from someone who sleeps in his bed. Every time you make me happy, shame punches me in the stomach, making me choke on my laughter. Everything I do with you stinks of betrayal. I know he isn't here anymore. But he will always live here. You cannot stay.

Even if you fight for me until your throat burns and your hands bleed. I will make you leave. I will lie to you about not loving you. Because lying is easier than loving.

WOLVES AND BUTTERFLIES

He grew up brave. He had to. He grew up with a sharp tongue to cut through any prejudice aimed at him. He learnt how to catch insults thrown at him, how to hurl them back with enough force to knock his opponent out with words.

He has spent years being told the butterflies in his stomach are just moths, eating away at the good part of his soul.

He is kind and brave and smart. But some people can't see that when he smells of another man's sheets.

Tonight, he is not calm. Tonight he is sweaty palms and nervous laughter and offering to pay the bill. It's like any other first date with mumbling and fixing his hair and excitement and first kissing. He can only see the man sitting in front of him. He is powerless when the man smiles.

Inside, at this table for two, everything is warm and the air is buzzing with butterflies.

But there are three wolves outside, circling and snapping their teeth. The streets are as dangerous as the woods and the wolves don't only come out at night here. They prowl the streets all hours, snarling about sin, as if they have any idea what it means. They howl at him and bar teeth. Their eyes are red and thirsty for blood. Its not human. It's a hate fuelled hunt for anything that doesn't smell like them.

It's the playground chant of "You are not like me and I don't like it." But it's not said with childish confusion. It's said with violent malice and fists. It's said with a centuries old hatred that the smarter minds of the world have outgrown.

The wolves are lead by a medieval believe that his love is less real and his feelings are less valid.

A goodnight kiss sends the butterflies wild. They form a hurricane in his stomach, knocking into his windpipe and making him dizzy.

The walk home should be a racing heart and delirious mind. He should be allowed his happiness. But the wolves are close behind, waiting for him to turn down the dark street. Not brave enough to attack in the light.

Then they strike. Screaming and snarling and clawing. They watched the blood hit the pavement as if they expected it to be different somehow – dirtier, muddier. But it was just red.

They use violence to try and kill love. They think they can punch it out of him.

They think they can crush his butterflies with their fists.

But his butterflies will always be his. They will always be real. They will always be the same as the butterflies everyone else has, they just have a different pattern on their wings.

LOVE LETTERS TO SICK PEOPLE

He clutched the note from his doctor in his bitten hands. He held onto it so tightly that the words could have transferred onto his skin. Sometimes he wished that he came with a written warning. Tattooed onto his arm, words that explained everything he hated to say out loud. Whenever he tried to explain it himself, it came out as an excuse instead of a reason. That's why the doctor's letter mattered. It was validation that everything was real. Sick not lazy, sick not lazy, sick not lazy. A knock on the door of his boss' office, a seat and a handshake. He handed over the paper and felt the relief run over his shoulders.

His boss read and re-read. "Ah. Well, I understand this is hard, but you're not really sick. Chin up boy, back to work."

He felt his skin crawl and his mind race. How could he explain what this feels like? How could he says that his mind felt like a graveyard, full of dead things he wanted to be dreams. It's grey and foggy and he can't remember the way out. The cracks in his mind had spread onto his body. He had starved it and overfed it worn it out.

He was screaming inside his head.

MY BRAIN IS SICK AND HAPPY THOUGHTS WILL NOT FIX IT.

Back to his desk, a seat and a computer.

His tie felt like it was strangling him. His palms were sweating and his ears burned. The room felt like it was spinning and his feet planted firmly on the floor did nothing to steady him.

He turned on his computer and watched data and numbers and charts open up. He tried to quieten the voice that was screaming in his ears – NONE OF THIS MATTERS. NOTHING MATTERS, NOTHING MATTERS, NOTHING MATTERS.

He typed words that he wish he could say – "I am terrified of becoming a ghost story. I am terrified of living as though I were dead."

He doesn't want sympathy. He wants someone to acknowledge the words his doctor wrote.

He wants to feel brave.

Someone needs to write him another letter. Someone needs to tell him the truth –

You are at your bravest on the days when you don't feel brave.

SAVING THE WORLD

She held her baby on one hip and shopping on the other. Carefully she carried him up five flights of stairs, filling both roles of what should have been a two persons job. Singing a lullaby, unaware of how strong her softness was.

She kissed his nose and sang him a song about stars and moons. He fell asleep in his second hand cot and he was the richest little boy in the world. She had painted animals on all the cracks on his walls. Staying up all night with a paintbrush, she had hidden the things she couldn't afford to repair with a whole kingdom of magical creatures. She told him about unicorns and dragons and all the things that lived in fairy tales.

Every second day she worked the night-shift at the supermarket, scrubbing the muddy footprints of people who were too important to avoid the wet bit of floor she had just mopped. As she pushed his pram to her sister's house before her shift began, she would notice the glances. People who were better than her wrinkled their noses as they looked at her hands – bright with fake tan and no ring on that finger. She earned disapproving whispers as she taught a human being how to be alive.

"So how old was she when she had him?!"

"How will he cope without a male figure in his life?"

"What kind of life will he have?"

The words "young single mother" come with such stigma when really, they should come with a cape. An appropriate reminder that superheroes are rarely rewarded with medals and movies. They usually just save the world quietly when no one is watching.

She was not a tragedy. She was not a sad story about loss or heart break. She was something fierce and powerful.

Even when her eyes were lined red with tiredness, she hit the alarm, put on her uniform and worked.

Some days you get up and don't realise that this day is going to be different, you can't tell if this will be a day you will remember for ever. One rainy morning she almost called in sick, as she had been up half the night with a restless baby. But she put on her cape and went to work.

As she finished mopping the filthy floor, she spun around as she heard someone sliding and falling down.

"Sorry," said the man as he stumbled to his feet. "I didn't mean to mess up your floor."

She recognised him, he only came into the shop every few days, early morning when most people were asleep. He wore pyjama bottoms and a shirt with a bow tie. She smiled at him, and the world changed.

THE HOUSE

This house doesn't have any windows or doors. You've been wandering through its derelict corridors for weeks, maybe months now. There is no clock, no calendar. You've lost all concept of how long you've been here. It's started to feel like home. The walls are lined with photographs of every moment of your life you wish you could forget. Every time you were hurt, every time you hurt someone. There are portraits of all the people you've lost. Their eyes move and stare at you when you walk by.

The lighting is poor, just bright enough for you to stumble your way through the halls but if you look too far ahead — everything just looks black.

When you first got here, you franticly fumbled, checking all your pockets for a key. Desperate for a way out. You lifted up every carpet, hoping to find a loose floorboard. You pushed every bookcase in case there was a secret passage. Every time, you became a little more defeated. Your steps got slower and you stopped hoping all together.

Now, you've grown so used to existing here that you've stopped considering leaving as an option. This is where you live.

It's such a big house for one person to live in alone. The walls creak and pipes groan and you feel like you're haunting it rather than living in it.

There are books here. All your favourite ones. But somehow, when you read them, they don't bring you joy like they used to.

This is a shadowy version of your life.

You don't belong here.

You were so busy clawing at the floorboards for a way out that you forgot to look up. There's an attic door. It seems far away but if you take a deep breath and reach your arm up, it's within touching distance.

You need to pull the door hard, and a little step ladder will fall down. The steps are rickety, they will feel unsafe and you might stumble. It's OK. One foot in front of the other, one at a time.

Start to climb them. Slowly stumble your way up the little ladder that, step by step, will lead you up. When you reach the top of the little ladder, look up again. You will see that the little ladder is actually a big ladder and it leads up to another door at the very very top of the house. Right onto the roof. Right onto the outside world that you haven't seen in so long. You stop. I know it feels easier to turn back. The steps look too high and there is no hand rail to steady you. You might fall. You need to know that there are people who love you outside. They have watched you live in this house for so long it's broken their hearts.

Do it slowly. One step at a time. If you trip and fall, knocking yourself back four steps, you can sit on the ground and curse yourself for a while. Then get back up. Start again.

That door on the roof will get closer and closer. After a few steps you can see it was never a far away as you though it was.

This is when you need to muster all the strength that you're not quite sure you have. Even if you don't believe you can do it, you must try. You will make it too the top no matter how many times you lose your footing. You will reach that door, push it open with every tiny little piece of bravery and strength you have.

Then, you can breathe as the air hits your face. You will feel your lungs filled with clear air. You will feel warmth gently prickle your skin as you pull yourself out of the house and into the daylight.

You will get out of here. You will see the sun again.

Erin May Kelly

THE MAN WHO LIVES UPSTAIRS

A letter fell through my door, addressed to the man upstairs. The one that children called "The Scarecrow." He had an unkempt look and was always alone. He rarely left his flat. He came outside to do his food shopping every second day. Always so early in the morning that most of the world around him was asleep.

So I took the letter to his front door. The man who lives upstairs is too young to be so resentful to the world, to have locked himself away from it already. He is going grey and looks older than he is.

I knocked three time and waited. There was a shuffling and a creak.

He wore a shirt and bow tie with pyjama bottoms and slippers — as if he was half ready to face the world and half never wanted to set foot in it again.

He let me in and it was like stepping into a black and white film. It was strange, like everything was faded, all his furniture was old and worn. It was as if someone had put a grey filter over all the bright colours. It felt like it was raining inside. There was a collection of ships in bottles and a fish tank with no fish.

After pouring me a tea, he sat back into his armchair and smiled.

He cleaned his glasses with a little green cloth and made small talk. He wasn't awkward or shy. He clearly knew how to interact with other people, he just didn't want to. He asked about my job and my husband and my holiday. I told him that I loved all three. I wanted to ask if he wanted a job or a partner or a holiday. But I didn't.

There were no photographs. The room we sat in was not spotless but not messy. There were so many little trinkets and ornaments, it looked like someone who had been on a lot of adventures lived here.

I glanced up, he had painted stars on the ceiling, like he was afraid he might forget what the night sky looked like. I felt like he was hibernating from a winter that had lasted years.

There was a map pinned to the wall behind him, with little red and blue dots of ink all over it.

He said the blue marked where he had been and the red was where he would go next.

I asked if he was lonely. He just smiled and said there were worse things to be than lonely.

I wondered if he knew the world wasn't ending. I tried joking, asking if he knew there wasn't an ongoing storm outside. It was safe out there — it's just full of people. He said there was a reason they name storms after people.

When I left, he closed the door. Locking himself back into his own little world.

TO MY DAUGHTER

There are some things you need to learn to make this world yours.

Nothing scares the world more than a girl who is unafraid. Sometimes history lessons make it seem like the world was built by men. Do your own research. Learn about all the women who screamed to have their voices heard and died for their rights.

Little girls grow into creatures than can hold human life in their bodies. Little girls grow into warriors that are immune to the sight of blood and learn how to deal with internal pain like it's nothing. When you grow up, you will be one of the strongest creatures on Earth, no matter how small you are.

You know how you learned that words can never hurt you? It's not true. People will craft sharp little insults to throw at you that sting no matter how hard you try to ignore them.

People will call you names if you kiss boys. People will call you names if you kiss girls. People will call you names if you don't kiss anyone. So just make sure you kiss whoever the Hell you want to.

Some people say that boys are mean to you because they like you. But if I teach you that the little boy who pulls your pigtails just does it because he likes you, then I'm teaching you that the man who hits you does it because he loves you. So whenever a boy pulls your hair, shove him off and find a boy who strokes your hair instead.

When you get older, men will say things to you that they think are compliments. Make sure you listen properly because sometimes insulting words are given in a pretty little box with a bow on top. Things like "You are so pretty, I prefer you without all that make up." Make sure he knows that your make up is not for him and you don't care what he prefers. Your look is yours and for your approval only.

I want you to know that you need to learn to snarl as well as whisper. Sometimes people will speak over you because your voice is soft. When that happens, just speak louder. Interrupt them like they interrupted you. Let them know that you are here to be heard and make your opinions impossible to ignore. You owe nothing to men you dance with in clubs. You owe nothing to men who buy you drinks. You owe your friends to leave with them safely at the end of the night.

You owe it to yourself to be heard, to be seen, and to be everything that you want.

THE SHORTEST STORY

This is the shortest story. This is the one I tried to write about you. I wanted metaphors about the stars and words so beautiful they would make you fall in love with me.
But there is no combination of words that could do you justice. So I'll just tell you this.
I always wanted to run away to the circus because it's magical, strange and incredible.
Then I met you. And you are magical and strange and incredible and suddenly, I didn't want to run away any more.

Erin May Kelly

BIOGRAPHY

Erin May Kelly is a Scottish writer, living in Edinburgh.

"The Everyday Circus" is her debut collection of short stories.

She is passionate about bringing to light subjects that can often get shied away from, such as mental health and domestic abuse. Her work is often built on a dark undertone but filled with hope when necessary.

You can find Erin and keep up to date with her writing news and more on her Facebook page.

Erin May Kelly

INDEX

Preface	5
Let's go down to the woods	7
Monsters	9
The Breakup Letter	13
Black Lungs	15
You after Him	17
Wolves and Butterflies	19
Love letters to sick people	21
Saving the world	23
The House	25
The man who lives upstairs	29
To my Daughter	31
The Shortest Story	33
Biography	35

ISBN : 978-1-911424-52-9
SKU/ID: 9781911424529
Publishing Company:
Black Wolf Edition & Publishing Ltd.
2 Glebe Place, Burntisland KY3 0ES, Scotland
www.blackwolfedition.com

Copyright © 2016 by Black Wolf Edition & Publishing Ltd.
All rights reserved. - First Printing: 2016
Second Edition 2017

www.ingramcontent.com/pod-product-compliance
Lightning Source LLC
Chambersburg PA
CBHW032045180726
48284CB00008B/2765